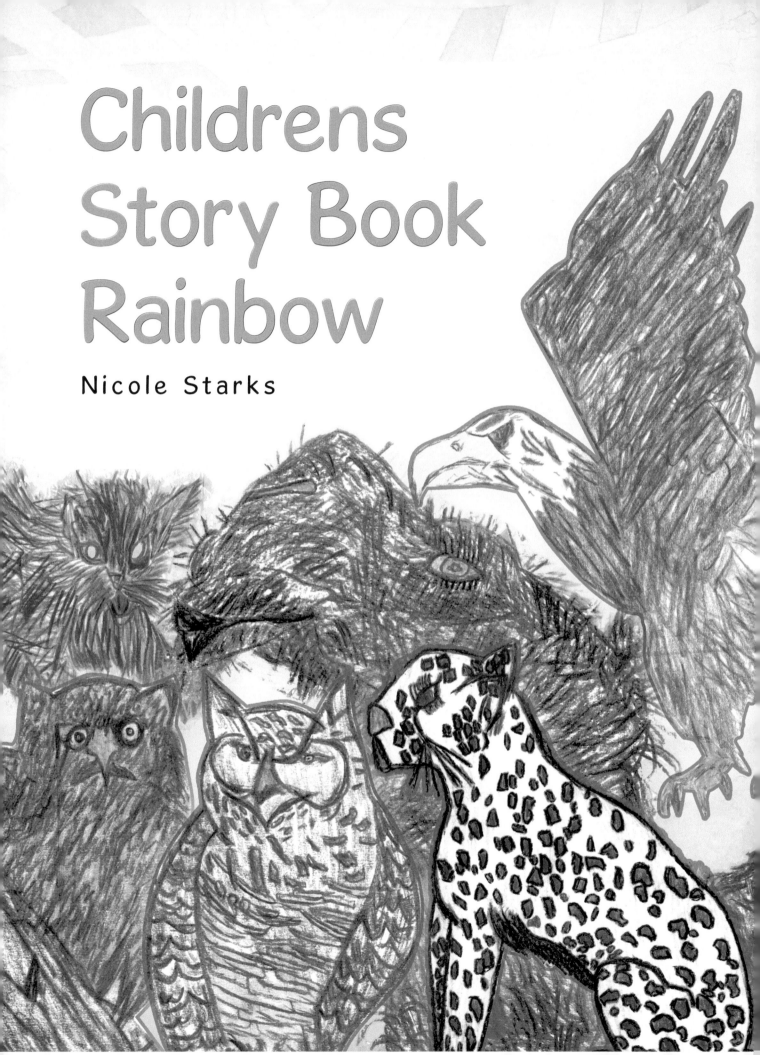

Childrens Story Book Rainbow

Nicole Starks

Order this book online at www.trafford.com
or email orders@trafford.com

Most Trafford titles are also available at major online book retailers.

Print information available on the last page.

ISBN: 978-1-4907-9491-4 (sc)
978-1-4907-9492-1 (e)

Our mission is to efficiently provide the world's finest, most comprehensive book publishing service, enabling every author to experience success. To find out how to publish your book, your way, and have it available worldwide, visit us online at www.trafford.com

Trafford rev. 04/24/2019

Trafford
PUBLISHING® www.trafford.com
North America & international
toll-free: 1 888 232 4444 (USA & Canada)
fax: 812 355 4082

Children Story Book Rainbow

By: Nicole Starks

Rest for Lee

Leeo is from Southern Los Angeles he has been a performer with other travelling circus leopards. Leeo at birth was a simple and quite young cub. He was chosen like the rest, to be a circus performer because of his loyalness to his family pack. When Leeo was choosen by a human ring circus master he noticed, Leeo had amazing strength. So off Leeo went for training, day after day turned into a year after year of warm cheers from the towns crowds. The ring maters most expensive chariots and traveling arrangements, Leeo even has a small circus of his own. Over the years his courage and strength, made lots of children and adults have special memories.

The end

Where Lorenzo and Business Went

Lorenzo and Business have been best owl friends since they hatched, being in a small forest and field like mill and barn, Lorenzo and Business always pictured a waterfall tropical grass and lots of acorns to eat. They both lifted their wings up at flight, from pine tree miles of oak trees and then finally the Redwood tree. Once Lorenzo and Business landed, they both purched on a strong huge branch and there was a waterfall, tall grass and lots of acorns.

The end

Fonzeez's Reflection

Fonzee lives in Arizona, it's quite a bright country for a small young kitten. Just taking a cat walk, Fonzee walks up and back and forth around a pond nearby. He gazed at the water until he noticed another kitten looking at him, it was his reflection.

The end

Fleease's Flight to Las Vegas

Fleease has flown over the Pacific Ocean many seas and has the strongest wings out at his breed. Fleease likes to float his strong wings through the wind. He's now ready to fly a more adventurous Flight so he sores to his right.

Swiftly and up glayding at full speed his eagles claws clenched up his beek brightened up the blue sky. He soared through the sky as strong as possible then, started to glayed. He's now at a new Desert Las Vegas.

The End

Jehounlaa's Palace

Jehounlaas is a famous wealthy camel, raised and chosen at birth by a very powerful king. He's the most accurate land organized camel herder, from desert to traveling around miles of oceans and large cities in Israel. Jehounlaa is dressed for festivals and never carries on her two camels humps any of the travelers, or their luggage food and water.

The king walks along side Jehounlaa very boldly passing through a small city in Israel. Jehounlaa slowly stops at her hind legs and the King looked at her face. He then knew this city in Israel is where Jehounlaa feels at peace.

Beenzo's

Beenzo is a small bear cub from, Tennessee his family pack is the usual hunter and bullies. They seem to know Beenzoo has a long way to go in the deep woods of Memphis. On the everyday family hunting, Beenzo trails very slowly amongst the other bears. Their prey are usually squirrels and foxes. Beenzo walks, until he's just close enough to a large May Flower tree, then stands heroically.

In the deep woods, his family is off to their daily food, leaving Beenzo. In their tracks and shadow, he has a change of pace, suddenly he returns back to walking. On all his front and hind legs Beenzo starts to become thirsty so he headed north swiftly, with a change of heart. His family always thought of him as their hero. Beenzo is very independent.

The deep woods made Beenzo want a New Forest trail, so he walked along side a perfect stream of water. To drink, eat fish, and rest by.

Finally, Beenzo found a New Home.

The End

Teetoe's

Teetoe is in Miami Florida. He enjoys to wag his tale, and the breeze of air that blows through his furried coat of hair. As he trouts about, suddenly a light crash of lightning and sound alerts Teetoe. Not very soon after that, the sky lit up in a quick flash. Teetoe, then paused and rain started to fall. Soon after a huge rainbow full of colors green, purple, orange, and tan yellow and pink.

The End

The Adventure of Cloudee

Cloudee is a mixed breed small puppy from Mexico, a village in Elpaso. On a summer day Cloudee wanted to follow the big bright Tuscan sun. He's fare and new, what an idea that Cloudee has, how can he make any trouble. The Glare made him curious, so Cloudee ended up not very far from the village. He troubled alongside a near stream bank of water.

The End

Printed in the United States
By Bookmasters